Flesh vs. Spirit Notebook

A Corrine Rios Ministries
Bible Study

In-Class Notes
Scriptural Memorization
Heartwork
Review Sheet
My Victory Plan

**For use while taking a Bible-Teacher
led Flesh vs. Spirit Bible Study.**

Table of Contents

Introduction

The Flesh vs. Spirit Bible Study is a self-confrontation Bible Study. We are commanded in 2 Corinthians 13:5, James 1:22-25, Lamentations 3:40, and in 1 Corinthians 11:28-32 to examine our ways. Self-examination, after salvation, to be able to function in the "new creation" we have become, once we gave our lives to Christ.

> *"Let us search out and examine our ways,*
> *And turn back to the Lord;*
> *Let us lift our hearts and hands*
> *To God in heaven."*
> **Lamentations 3:40-41**

We need to exam ourselves according to God's Word. Then we will know how short we have fallen. We need obedience to Ephesians 4:22-24, "that you put off, concerning your former conduct, the old man which grows corrupt according to the deceitful lusts, and be renewed in the spirit of your mind, and that you put on the new man which was created according to God, in true righteousness and holiness." We use this as the ultimate model in overcoming sin, death, and the Devil so that we can function in the "new creation."

We need to "put off" functioning in the misdeeds of the flesh by "putting on" the Holy Spirit so that we can be used to spread the Gospel and LIVE an abundant life, John 10:10.

"I say then: Walk in the Spirit, and you shall not fulfill the lust of the flesh."
Galatians 5:16

"I can do all things through Christ who strengthens me."
Philippians 4:13

"But put on the Lord Jesus Christ, and make no provision for the flesh, to fulfill its lusts."
Romans 13:14

"Finally, my brethren, be strong in the Lord and in the power of His might. Put on the whole armor of God, that you may be able to stand against the wiles of the devil."
Ephesians 6:10-11

In this Bible Study, you will learn HOW TO be IN His Spirit.

If you have purchased this Flesh vs. Spirit Notebook that means you are, hopefully, taking a Flesh vs. Spirit Bible Study. This notebook includes the In-Class Notes, Scripture Memorization, Heartwork (homework), Review Sheet, and My

Victory Plan Instructions. This notebook is meant to be used as you take the eleven week Bible Study with a Bible Teacher. As the teacher teaches each lesson, you will be directed to your Notebook (In-Class Notes) to look over or fill in the blanks.

The Notebook is a quick reference of Scriptural Principles and HOW TO Principles taught in each lesson. Please bring it to every lesson.

Each lesson in this Notebook has its own separate book for purchase. The In-Class Notes, Scripture Memorization, Heartwork, Review Sheet, and My Victory Plan Instructions are included with each individual purchase of the Flesh vs. Spirit Series. You do not need to buy the Notebook Book if you purchase books one through eleven.

This Notebook can be used when you are discipling others. Use it as a reference for the various problems people are facing.

In-Class Notes
Lesson 1: Deny Self Understanding God's Focus For Our Living

The Purpose: this lesson will give Biblical understanding of how we are functioning, either in our flesh or in His Spirit. We will learn God's focus for our living and how to overcome a preoccupation with self.

Ephesians 5:29	2 Timothy 3:1-5
Matthew 22:37-40	Luke 9:23-24
1 Corinthians 2:12-14	Colossians 3:2
Psalm 24:1	Mark 10:45
1 Peter 4:10-11	Psalm 121
Galatians 5:17-23	Romans 8:5-13
Matthew 7:12	2 Corinthians 5:17
Psalm 37:4-5	

SP-Scriptural Principle   HP–HOW TO Principle

SP1 Ephesians 5:29 and 2 Timothy 3:1-5 - The natural man (self).

1-1) MY view of self affects how I approach ALL problems in my life.

SP2 2 Timothy 3:1-5 The natural man pays too much attention to self, not too little.

1-2) 2 Timothy 3:1-5 My problems are because I pay too much attention to self, not too little.

SP3 Matthew 22:37-40 To love and overcome my problems, I need only to reverse my focus from myself to God and others.

1-3) I cannot follow Jesus, if I do not deny self/die to self.

SP4 Luke 9:23-24, Mark 8:34-35, Matthew 16:24-25 God's focus for living should also be my focus for living; deny self, carry my cross daily, and follow Him.

Has this been your focus for living in every situation and with every person?

1-4) God has created me to love, like He loves me.

1-5) I am not responsible for my feelings, they are involuntary BUT I am responsible for my THOUGHTS, WORDS, and ACTIONS. Strong feelings are an indication that the FLESH wants to make an appearance.

1-6) When I take my perceived needs (SELF) out of the equation, I have His Spirit of love. I can see the other person the way God sees that person instead of what I think I need in that moment. I can see the circumstances in my life as an opportunity to grow.

1-7) I was created in LOVE, to function in LOVE, to show LOVE. WHEN I function the way I was created, I will experience the fruit of the Spirit. (Galatians 5:22-23)

1-8) A dead body (that has died to self), cannot be hurt.

HOW TO deny self - Think Differently:

HP1 1 Corinthians 2:16, Colossians 3:2 How I think determines what I think.

HP2 Psalm 24:1 God has given me everything I have. Everything I have belongs to HIM.

1-9) I am a steward (managing partner with God) of everything I have because God has given me all I have.

<u>HOW TO deny self</u> - Serve Others:

HP3 Mark 10:45, 1 Peter 4:10-11 Jesus came to serve. I must also serve others.

1-10) I am to serve others with the gift God has given me.

<u>HOPE:</u> Psalm 121

1-11) WHEN _____ function the way _____ was created, **THEN** _____ will have love, joy, peace, patience, kindness, goodness, gentleness, faithfulness, and self-control spilling out of me. Galatians 5:22-25

1-12) WHEN God commands that _____ deny self, carry my cross daily and follow Him, **THEN** He has given ME the ability to do so!

<u>Notes</u>

Scriptural Memorization

"Your word I have treasured in my heart, That I may not sin against You." Psalm 119:11

"Let the word of Christ richly dwell within you, with all wisdom teaching and admonishing one another with psalms and hymns and spiritual songs, singing with thankfulness in your hearts to God." Colossians 3:16

Scriptural Memorization is the Christian's tool in having victory over the temptation to sin. When you have His Word implanted in your heart, He will bring them into your remembrance when you are in trials. When you memorize His Word you are well equipped to have VICTORY in your life. The following are great verses to memorize.

Scriptural Principles to memorize:

Matthew 22:37-40   2 Timothy 3:1-5
Ephesians 5:29
Galatians 5:22-25

HOW TO Deny Self Principles to memorize:

Luke 9:23-24   Mark 10:45
Psalm 24:1   1 Peter 4:10-11

<u>Heartwork</u>

1) How does God view natural man (self)? Write out the verses

2) How do we turn from "such people" if we are "such people"? Site verse and then explain in your own words.

3) Why does your view of self affect how you approach all problems in life?

4) What verse shows us that we are to put on a preoccupation of God and others before ourselves? Write out Matthew 22:37-39.

5) How did God create us?

6) What benefits do we get when we function the way we were created?

7) What ways, in your daily life, have you failed to "deny self"? Be specific. Think about your thoughts, words, and actions.

8) What is God leading you to change this semester?

9) Look at different Bible versions of 2 Timothy 3:1-5, suggested NKJV, NIV, NLT, AMP, MSG. Write down your favorite verse version.

10) Explain what "a dead body cannot be hurt" means.

11) What are the two ways to "deny self"?

12) What are your Spiritual gifts?

13) Why do all our problems in our horizontal relationship indicate a problem in our vertical relationship?

Expanded Bible Study

*When you have "strong emotions/feelings", stop and think about the way you will react. Either in the flesh or Spirit.

*Research how many times "deny self" in mentioned in the Bible.

*Put checkmarks on 2 Timothy 3:1-5

*Write some Scripture on index cards-ones that HE is leading you to renew your mind with to help you understand and/or put off a preoccupation with self.

In-Class Notes
Lesson 2: How Do I Put Off My Angry Reactions?

The Purpose: this lesson will show that human anger does not produce the Godly behaviors that God desires for us. When we sin in our anger we are showing God and others that we are not functioning in His Spirit. This lesson also introduces the ONLY method for overcoming any temptation to sin.

James 4:17	John 13:17
Jeremiah 17:9	Galatians 5:19-20, 6:4-5
Colossians 3:8-14	James 1:19-20
1 Corinthians 2:16	Colossians 3:2
Mark 7:15, 11:15-18	Ephesians 5:1, 4:22-24
James 1:22-25	1 Corinthians 10:13
Galatians 5:22-23	1 Peter 2:21-23

SP - Scriptural Principle   HP – HOW TO Principle

SP5 James 4:17 (NIV) "If anyone, then, knows the good they ought to do and doesn't do it, it is sin for them."

SP6 John 13:17 (NIV) "Now that I know these things, you will be blessed if do them."

2-1) How does your anger manifest (look like)? The usual manifestations of anger are sinful thoughts, cussing, yelling at others, and hitting. However, other behaviors can include giving the silent treatment, running away, or not doing for others what you normally do.

2-2) In Mark 11:15-17, Jesus's anger was justified because:

      a) Jesus had the proper **motivation**

      b) Jesus had the proper **focus.**

      c) Jesus had the proper **supplement.**

      d) Jesus had the proper **control.**

      e) Jesus had the proper **duration.**

      f) Jesus had the proper **result.**

      g) Can human anger be justified? _____.

2-3) How can I know if my anger is sinful. (Checkmark all that apply).

____ I am quick tempered or have angry outbursts. (Galatians 5:20, Ephesians 4:31, James 1:19).

____ I become angry, am not merciful, compassionate, and forgiving. (Nehemiah 9:17, Psalm 86:15, Ephesians 4:32).

____ I seek vengeance or retaliation against another. (Romans 12:17-19, Hebrews 10:30).

_____ I violate Biblical love in my anger. (1 Corinthians 13:4-8, 1 Peter 4:8).

_____ I fail to demonstrate the fruit of the Spirit in my thoughts, words, and actions, especially self-control. (Galatians 5:22).

_____ I use words that are not edifying. (Matthew 12:36-37, Ephesians 4:29, 1 Peter 3:10).

_____ I respond angrily in order to "protect your rights" or "get your own way". (Luke 9:23, 2 Corinthians 5:15, 1 Peter 2:21-23).

_____ I have an abiding (continuing) anger against another (Matthew 5:21-22) or let the sun go down on your anger. (Ephesians 4:25).

_____ I respond to anger in a manner that does not please the Lord (2 Corinthians 5:9, Colossians 1:10) or does not bring honor to His name.

_____ I become angry and neglect to rejoice, to pray, or to give thanks in the very situation I find myself in (1 Thessalonians 5:16-18)." Biblical Counseling Foundation, Self-Confrontation

Draw two bottles; one fleshy and one pure water (His Spirit). Circle the bottle that you want coming out of you.

Is anger in your heart? _____

SP7 Jeremiah 17:9 Only what is in my heart can come out when shaken. My angry reactions to people and circumstances only reveal what is in my heart already

SP8 Galatians 5:19-20, Colossians 3:8, James 1:19-20
People who are quickly aroused or quickly express anger or bitterness have a strong preoccupation with self and are in sin.

SP9 Mark 7:15 "Hear Me, everyone, and understand: There is nothing that enters a man from outside which can defile him; but the things which come out of him, those are the things that defile a man." Mark 7:15. Nothing and no one can make you react in anger.

2-4) Anger has two components: **Feelings and deeds.**
       a) Feelings are involuntary. I am not responsible for them.
       b) Deeds I am responsible for.
       c) Deeds are thoughts, words, and actions. TWA

2-5) My love for God and others are inseparable. I show my love for God by how I treat others. How are you treating others?

HOW TO Put Off My Angry Reactions

HP4 1 Corinthians 2:16, Colossians 3:2 How I think about my anger determines what I think.

HP5 Mark 7:15 I am the reason I am angry. No one can make me sin in my anger.

HP6 Ephesians 4:22-24 "Put off, renew, put on" Do your Victory Plan. (Instructions found on page 125).

- ➤ 1st Column   Self-examine - 1 Corinthians 11:28
- ➤ 2nd Column   Put offs - Ephesians 4:22
- ➤ 3rd Column   Put ons - Ephesians 4:23-24
- ➤ 4th Column   Make a plan - Titus 2:11-14

   DO YOUR PLAN!! James 1:22-25

<u>**HOPE:**</u> 1 Corinthians 10:13

2-6) WHEN God **COMMANDS** me not to sin in my anger, **THEN** God gives me the ability to do so.

2-7) WHEN I function the way I was created, **THEN** I will have love, joy peace, patience, kindness, gentleness, goodness, faithfulness, and _____. (Fill in blank) Galatians 5:22-25

<u>NOTES</u>

Scriptural Memorization

"Your word I have treasured in my heart, That I may not sin against You." Psalm 119:11

"Let the word of Christ richly dwell within you, with all wisdom teaching and admonishing one another with psalms and hymns and spiritual songs, singing with thankfulness in your hearts to God." Colossians 3:16

Scriptural Memorization is the Christian's tool in having victory over the temptation to sin. When you have His Word implanted in your heart, He will bring them into your remembrance when you are in trials. When you memorize His Word you are well equipped to have VICTORY in your life. The following are great verses to memorize.

Scriptural Principles to memorize:

James 4:17	John 13:17
Psalm 66:18	Isaiah 59:1-2
Jeremiah 17:9	

HOW TO Put Off My Anger Principles:

Ephesians 4:22-24 (ultimate HOW TO verse)
James 1:19-20
Colossians 3:8-14

Heartwork

1) Write out Jeremiah 17:9. In your own words, what does it mean?

2) "Only what is in your heart can come out." What does that mean?

3) What comes out of you when shaken?

4) What reaction(s) would you like to change?

5) Why is it important to have a Spiritual Plan for long lasting Biblical New Creation Functioning?

6) Explain the steps and provide Scriptural References for having victory over our failures. (found on the My Victory Plan)

7) Explain what each verse means.

Ephesians 4:22-24   1 Corinthians 11:28   Titus 2:11-14
Colossians 3:5-9   Colossians 3:10-17

8) Give at least two "put off" and "put on" verses about anger.

9) Is human anger ever justified? Why? Why not?

10) Do you have some work to do in regards to your angry thoughts, words, and actions?

11) Why does putting off your angry reactions involve "denying self"?

12) Fill out a My Victory Plan Sheet and start using it. Instructions found on page 125.

My Victory Plan Over Sin, Death, and the Devil

Through the death and resurrection of the Lord Jesus Christ, God was victorious over SIN (Romans 6:10), DEATH (Romans 6:9), and the DEVIL (Hebrews 2:15).

Ephesians 4:22-24

Self-examine 1 Corinthians 11:28, Galatians 6:4	Put off Eph. 4:22	Put on Eph. 4:23-24	MY PLAN Titus 2:11-14
List specific unbiblical T,W,A- not just emotions or attitudes	For each pattern of sin, write one or two verses as a "put off"	List specific biblical verses for each sinful pattern	List SPECIFIC T,W,A that will replace column 1

In-Class Notes
Lesson 3: How Do I Forgive Like God Forgives Me?

The Purpose: in this lesson we discover how God forgives us. It is with this model of forgiveness that we are to forgive others.

Romans 12:18	1 John 4:20-21
Nehemiah 9:16-17	Psalm 103:10-12
Ephesians 4:29-31	1 Corinthians 13:5
Philippians 4:6-9	Hebrews 10:17
2 Corinthians 2:6-8	Galatians 5:22-26
Matthew 18:35	Psalm 66:18
Isaiah 59:2	Isaiah 43:25
James 2:10	Mark 11:25-26
Matthew 5:23	Matthew 5:43-44
1 Peter 3:8-9	John 7:24

SP – Scriptural Principle   HP – HOW TO Principle

SP10 Romans 12:18 "If it is possible, as much as depends on you, live peacefully with all men."

So far, from what we have learned in this Bible Study, what is dependent on you.

    a) Deny self, carry my cross daily, and follow HIM
    b) Put off my anger and bitterness
    c) AND today we add: Forgive and be reconciled

3-1) If I love God but hate my brother by not regarding them before myself AND/OR have anger or bitterness towards them AND/OR have un-forgiveness toward them, I am NOT really loving God. 1 John 4:20-21

3-2) What does my unforgiveness look like?

_____

3-3) Lack of true Godly forgiveness is so serious that if, I, a believer, do not forgive others, God will not forgive me (I will not have the joy of my salvation).

3-4) God's forgiveness:
    a) God is ready to forgive compassionate, gracious, slow to anger, abounding in love. Nehemiah 9:16-17
    b) God forgives ALL sins.
    c) God removes ALL sins from me. Psalm 103:11-12
    d) God does not to hold my sin against me. Psalm 103
    e) God's forgiveness includes kindness and tenderness. Ephesians 4:31
    f) God remembers my sin no more. Jeremiah 31:34
    g) God blots out my sin and will never think of them again. Isaiah 43:25

Does my forgiveness look like God's? _____

If not, I have some work to do in this area.

From the Scriptures you learned, does God command we forgive ourselves? Are there any verses in the Bible that command us to forgive ourselves?

SP11 Nehemiah 9:16-17, Psalm 103:11-12, Ephesians 4:31
God forgave ALL sins in my life. I should be willing to forgive the relatively FEW sins committed against me.

3-5) It is possible and expected by God, that I do not hold the offense against the offender. When I hold the offense against the offender, I stay stuck in unforgiveness.

How do I hold the offenses of others against them?

> a) Continue to think about their offenses
> b) Ignore them (silent treatment)
> c) Gossip/slander about them
> d) Run away
> c) Have angry thoughts, words, or actions when you see them
> d) Other _____

3-6) Continuing to focus (in an accusing way) on what the person did is a sign that I am still holding it against him and haven't forgiven God's way.

3-7) In order to know if the offense is a sin, you need to make a righteous judgment about it. "Stop judging by mere appearances, but instead judge correctly." John 7:24

3-8) Unforgiveness and treating others as their sins deserve is a sign that you want to avenge yourself. Avenge means to punish the wrongdoer responsible for the sin.

3-9) What are you really trying to do when you hold the offense against the offender? You are punishing the offender. Is that your job? Whose job is it?

3-10) Forgiveness is possible even for the gravest of offenses, through the power of the Holy Spirit.

SP12 Scriptural Forgiveness principles (taken from the Biblical Counseling Foundation, Self-Confrontation Book)

- "Forgiveness is an act of obedience to the Lord (Luke 17:3-10, Ephesians 4:32, Colossians 3:13) and must be granted from the heart. (Matthew 18:35) **BEFORE** asked and/if **NEVER** asked.
- Forgiveness gives the offender what he needs rather than what he deserves (Psalm 103:10, Romans 5:8). What do we deserve? Death

- Forgiveness should include comforting those who have sinned and have repented, as well as reaffirming my love to them by not repaying evil for evil. (II Corinthians 2:5-8)
- Forgiveness is to be granted without limits. Matthew 18:21-22" Biblical Counseling Foundation, Self-Confrontation

HOW TO Forgive Like God Forgives Me:

If someone sins against you...

HP7 Mark 11:25-26, Matthew 18:35 If someone sins against you, you are to forgive immediately by doing **HP8 – 14 (below).** You are not asked to have those feelings of forgiveness, you are commanded to "show" forgiveness. The feelings of forgiving others will come as you DO.

"Forgiveness is the love of Jesus Christ in action and is an act of my will and a commitment to:

HP8 Matthew 5:43-44 "You have heard that it was said, 'You shall love your neighbor and hate your enemy.' But I say to you, love your enemies, **bless** those who curse you, **do good** to those who hate you, and **pray** for those who spitefully use you and persecute you," Those who are sinning against us, because of their behavior, can be considered our enemy-they are working against us in that time of their ungodly actions toward us. **PUT OFF:** hating your enemy, **PUT ON:** love by blessing, doing good, and praying for them.

HP9 1 Peter 3:8-9 "Finally, all of you be of one mind, having **compassion** for one another; love as brothers, be tenderhearted, be courteous; not returning evil for evil or reviling for reviling, but on the contrary **blessing**, knowing that you were called to this, that you may inherit a blessing." **PUT OFF:** not returning evil or evil or reviling for reviling **PUT ON:** love by compassion, tenderhearted, courteous, blessings.

HP10 NOT keep a record of wrongs. 1 Corinthians 13:5 (thoughts)

HP11 NOT gossip about a person's sins. Ephesians 4:29 (speech)

HP12 NOT dwell on the offense yourself. Philippians 4:8 (thoughts)

HP13 NOT bring up or remind a person of their sin in an accusing manner. Hebrews 10:17 (words). We do this by treating others as if they **never committed the sin in the first place.**

These are excellent for your Victory Plan.

When you have completely forgiven the one who sinned against you, you will be able to treat that person as you always have.

You are reconciled with God AND with that person. Restoring that relationship is different than reconciliation.

HOW TO be reconciled with others:

If someone is NOT treating you like they always have, you may have feelings of being mad/upset/angry at them. You then have "something against them."

HP7 Forgive anyone who has sinned against you. In this case, they aren't treating you like they usually do.

HP15 Matthew 5:23 If someone has something against you, you are to go be reconciled. Reconciliation means the end of the estrangement. You are trying to find out why the estrangement. "I sense some tension between us; did I do something to offend you?" LISTEN

HP14 RESTORE fellowship with the forgiven person or the offender, as far as biblically possible. Romans 12:18, II Corinthians 2:6-8 (actions). The Lord may not want the relationship restored.

HOW TO do your part in restoring a relationship:

HP7 Forgive anyone who has sinned against you. Restoring means the returning of something or someone to their original state.

HP15 Go be reconciled if someone has something against you. Not all relationships can be restored.

HP16 – John 15:12-13 "My command is this: Love each other as I have loved you. Greater love has no one than this: to lay down one's life for one's friends." Continue to deny self with this person. You are to treat them **AS IF the sin was never committed.** "If it is possible, as much as depends on you, live peaceably with all men." Do your part. The other person has a part in the relationship. If they aren't doing their part, the relationship cannot be restored. You may have to put on Biblical Boundaries. More in Lesson 9.

3-11) Unwillingness to forgive and be reconciled is an indication of pride, not an inability. I am living to please myself when I do not show forgiveness. When I live to please myself, I am NOT loving God and NOT loving my neighbor as myself.

3-12) Forgiveness without denying self and putting off anger and bitterness is not true Biblical forgiveness.

<u>**HOPE:**</u> Galatians 6:8

3-13) **WHEN** God commands me to forgive others, **THEN** God has given me the ability to do so.

3-14) **WHEN** I function the way I was created, **THEN** I will have love, joy, peace, patience, kindness, gentleness, goodness, _____, and _____. Galatians 5:22-25

<u>Notes</u>

Scriptural Memorization

"Your word I have treasured in my heart, That I may not sin against You." Psalm 119:11

"Let the word of Christ richly dwell within you, with all wisdom teaching and admonishing one another with psalms and hymns and spiritual songs, singing with thankfulness in your hearts to God." Colossians 3:16

Scriptural Memorization is the Christian's tool in having victory over the temptation to sin. When you have His Word implanted in your heart, He will bring them into your remembrance when you are in trials. When you memorize His Word you are well equipped to have VICTORY in your life. The following are great verses to memorize.

Scriptural Principles to Memorize:

Matthew 18:35   Psalm 103:10-12
Isaiah 43:25

HOW TO Forgive Like God Forgives Me Principles:

Mark 11:25-26   Matthew 5:43-44
Matthew 5:23   1 Peter 3:8-9

Heartwork

1) Finish this statement: _____ am not loving God when I refuse to forgive others.

2) According to God, do you need an apology to grant forgiveness?

3) Is there someone in your life that has something against you?

4) What does God command of you when you know this? Site the Scripture.

5) In your own words, what does this Scripture mean?

6) Briefly write about how you can be a peacemaker in this situation.

7) What two ways does God forgive us? Site Scripture

8) Look at the Forgiveness Principles and write down the ones you need to work on in granting Biblical Forgiveness.

9) After learning how God wants us to forgive, is there anyone in your life that you thought you'd forgiven but realize you really hadn't? Look at the Forgiveness Principles....

!0) With all that you have learned so far, do you agree with this statement? Helping others solve their problems biblically requires that I deal with that person's relationship with the Lord and his/her subsequent obedience in practicing biblical love in all of his/her relationships. Why or Why not?

11) If you need to forgive someone, fill out a My Victory Plan and do it.

12) Will God always restore a relationship when only one party is willing to be reconciled to the Lord?

In-Class Notes
Lesson 4: How Do I Love Like Jesus Regardless of How I Feel?

The Purpose: in this lesson we discover, or rediscover, God's definition of love and what that should look like in our lives. God commands us to show love to everyone, even if we do not feel like it.

Matthew 22:36-40	Luke 6:27-30
Matthew 12:36	1 Corinthians 13:4-8
Luke 6:45	John 1:9
Matthew 18:15-17	James 3:2-6
John 13:34-35	Romans 14:12-23
John 15:12	Proverbs 19:11b
1 Corinthians 6:9-10	Ephesians 4:15

SP - Scriptural Principles   HP – HOW TO Principles

SP13 Matthew 22:36-40 "Teacher, which is the great commandment in the law?" Jesus said to him, "You shall love the Lord your God with all your heart, with all your soul, and with all your mind.' This is the first and great commandment. And the second is like it: You shall love his/her neighbor as him/herself. On these two commandments hang all the Law and the Prophets."

4-1) Three kinds of human love described in Bible: **storge** (parental), **eros** (erotic) **phileo** (brotherly). ONE kind of God's love **AGAPE** (self-sacrificial). The Greek word agape is often translated "love" in the New Testament. Agape love is always shown by what it does.

4-2) God's love is:

a) **Supernatural** – 1 John 4:8 "He who does not love does not KNOW God, for God is love." God is a Spirit

b) **Unconditional** – Romans 5:8 "But God demonstrates His own love toward us, in that while we were still sinners, Christ died for us."

c) **Other's Centered** – Mathew 22:39 "and the second is like it: 'You shall love your neighbor as yourself."

d) **Hopeful** - Romans 5:5 "Now hope does not disappoint, because the love of God has been poured out in our hearts by the Holy Spirit who was given to us." **Therefore, God's love is…**

e) **SACRIFICIAL – John 3:16 "He gave us His one and only Son to die for us."**

4-3) The primary meaning of the word "love" in Scriptures is a purposeful commitment of sacrificial action for another. This includes; my brothers, my neighbors, my children, my ex's, my enemies.

4-4) Biblical love towards others is an act of MY will in obedience to GOD and is not dependent on MY feelings or the actions of others.

4-5) ALL of God's commands for living are based on these verses of loving God and loving others in a biblical manner.

SP14 Luke 6:27-30 Right feelings FOLLOW right actions. Loving our enemies is not a natural thing to do. God isn't telling you to "feel" like you love your enemies. He is commanding you to have loving actions toward them. Loving actions are your thoughts, words, and physical deeds.

SP15 1 Corinthians 13:4-8 This is God's measuring stick. He judges/blesses us according to how we are loving others according to 1 Corinthians 13:4-8. How we love others shows our love for God. Love is tested when I am shaken AND when I do not feel like being loving.

4-6) Biblical love ALLOWS God to use the earthly consequences for correction.

4-7) _____ (My) words, _____ (my) tone, and _____ (my) attitude in which _____ (I) speak are critical to peaceful relationships.

4-8) The power of MY words is enormous and they also show the condition of my heart. One of our biggest failures is how we communicate with one another.

4-9) My idle words will be accounted for in the Day of Judgment. The Greek word "argos" (translated as "idle") – means "inactive, unfruitful, barren, lazy, useless, or unprofitable. Matthew 12:36

4-10) As _____ (I) learn to speak the truth in love, _____ (I) must also determine:

    a) When to speak
    b) How to speak in an edifying manner
    c) To Whom I should speak
    d) What to speak

4-11) "What do MY words reveal?

    a) My words are a mirror of MY heart. (Luke 6:45)

    b) My words reflect MY intent to heal or to hurt.
        (Proverbs 11:9, 11, 12:18)

    c) My words are indicators of MY spiritual maturity
        (Ecclesiastes 10:12-14, and in James 3:1- 6)

    d) My words reveal a self-focus (by cursing) or a focus
        on God and others (by blessing). (James 3:9-
        12, I Peter 3:8-10)

4-12) What do my unloving ways look like? _____

_____

_____

HOW TO communicate Biblically:

HP17 To **whom should I speak? (fill in with I)**

   a) Speak with God first so that _____ understand
      His truth. (James 1:5)
   b) Speak to_____ next, to determine the changes
      _____ may need to make. (Matthew 7:1-5)
   c) Speak to the wise, not to the foolish scoffer.
      (Proverbs 9:7- 9, 19:25; 23:9)
   d) Speak to the receptive, not to the quarrelsome.
      (Proverbs 17:14, 20:3) Speak only to those who
      need to know. (Proverbs 11:13-14)
   e) Speak to those who need hope, comfort, restoration
      or regeneration (spiritual new birth). (Matthew
      28:19-20, II Corinthians 1:3-4, 5:18-20, I Peter
      3:15)

HP18 **When should I speak?**

   a) _____ should speak after gathering the facts
      (Proverbs 18:13)
   b) _____ need to listen attentively, rather than
      concentrating on what I am going to say
      (Proverbs10:19, 15:28, 18:2)

c) _____ need to listen to all sides, don't jump to conclusion (based on Proverbs 18:13, 17)

d) _____ need to speak AFTER thinking (Proverbs 13:3, 15:28, James 1:19)

e) _____need to speak at the appropriate time (Proverbs 15:23, 25:11)

HP19 How to speak:

a) _____ am to speak with control over my emotions. (Proverbs 15:1, 16:32: 17:27)

b) _____ am to speak w/o quarreling (Proverbs 17:14, 20:3)

c) _____ am to speak with sweetness, gentleness, graciousness, and reverence (Colossians 4:6, I Peter 3:15) and yet with confidence and authority. (Titus 2:15, 3:8)

d) _____ am to speak with a blessing in response to insults (Proverbs 20:22, Romans 12:14, 1 Peter3:9)

e) _____ am to speak in an manner that is acceptable and pleasing to God (Psalm 19:14)

HP20 What I should NOT say:

a) _____ should not lie. (Deuteronomy 5:20, Proverbs 4:24, Ephesians 4:25)

b) _____ should not use words that are unwholesome, slanderous, malicious, or abusive, since these are practices of the old self. (Ephesians 4:29)

c) _____ should not curse or speak with bitterness since these are signs of wickedness and unrighteousness. (Psalm 10:2-11)

d) _____ should not speak in silly, joking, or coarse manner since this is not fitting behavior for a child of God. (Ephesians 5:4)

e) _____ should avoid worldly and empty chatter since this leads to further ungodliness. (I Timothy 6:20, II Timothy 2:16)

HP21 What **should I speak?**

a) _____ should always speak the truth. (Ephesians 4:15)

b) _____ should speak God's words rather than my own opinions or man's philosophies. (Proverbs 30:5-6, Isaiah 55:8-11) You are not the authority.

c) _____ should speak wholesome words that give grace to those who hear. (Proverbs 15:1, Ephesians 4:29, Colossians 4:6).

d) _____ should speak with a view to reconcile others to the Lord. (II Corinthians 5:20)

e) _____ should speak to give witness for the Lord. (I Peter 3:15)

f) _____ should speak in thanksgiving (Psalm 9:1) and praise to the Lord (Psalm 145:1-7, 150:1-6)" Biblical Counseling Foundation

4-12) Biblical love and communication is an act of _____ (my) will in obedience to God and is not dependent on my feelings or how others treat me.

HOPE: Isaiah 43:1-2

4-13) WHEN God _____ me to love others, regardless of my feelings, **THEN** God has given _____ the _____ to do so.

4-14) WHEN I _____ the way I was _____, **THEN** _____ will have love, joy, peace, patience, kindness, goodness,
_____,
_____, and
_____ spilling out of me regardless of how I am feeling. Galatians 5:22-25

<u>Notes</u>

Scriptural Memorization

"Your word I have treasured in my heart, That I may not sin against You." Psalm 119:11

"Let the word of Christ richly dwell within you, with all wisdom teaching and admonishing one another with psalms and hymns and spiritual songs, singing with thankfulness in your hearts to God." Colossians 3:16

Scriptural Memorization is the Christian's tool in having victory over the temptation to sin. When you have His Word implanted in your heart, He will bring them into your remembrance when you are in trials. When you memorize His Word you are well equipped to have VICTORY in your life. The following are great verses to memorize.

Scriptural Principles to Memorize:

Matthew 22:36-40   1 Corinthians 13:4-8

HOW TO Love Regardless of How I Feel Principles:

Pick the ones you need work on from HP17-21 (pgs. 40-43)

<u>Heartwork</u>

1) What is the meaning of Biblical love? Write out the verse

2) What are some ways that you did not/do not show biblical love in your thoughts, words, or actions?

3) What do your words reveal about yourself?

4) Give at least one Scripture References for each:

Who should we speak to?

When should we speak?

How should we speak?

What should we speak?

5) Ask God for guidance on this next task:

Ask God to reveal to you, how you have failed at communicating biblically. Write out the specific incident(s). And how you can be right with God.

6) Fill out a My Victory Plan. Instructions found on page 125

In-Class Notes
Lesson 5: How Do I Have a Godly Marriage?

The Purpose: this lesson focuses on submissiveness. We will learn how Jesus was submissive to His Father. Men and women are to be submissive to God and then to each other like Jesus was submissive to His Father.

> **Submission:** James 4:7, Romans 13:1-7, Hebrews 13:17, 1 Peter 3:13-14, Titus 3:1, Ephesians 5:21-24, 1 Peter 5:5
>
> **God Ordained Marriage:** Genesis 2:23-24, Genesis 2:18-20, Matthew 19:6
>
> **Contentious Spirit:** Proverbs 10:12, 25:24, 28:25, Ephesians 4:31, Philippians 2:14, Proverbs 28:25
>
> **Marriage Verses:** Ephesians 5:18-33, 1 Peter 3:1-17
>
> **Maintenance:** Proverbs 19:11, 17:9, 10:12

SP - Scriptural Principle   HP – HOW TO Principle

5-1) There are few verses in the Bible about marriage in particular. The hundreds of verses focusing on your personal walk with Christ, whether single or married, illustrate the primary focus of God's Word.

5-2) Biblical submission is an act of my will demonstrated by my serving others out of an attitude that regards them as more important than myself.

SP16 1 Peter 2:21-25 Jesus is _____ example, _____ am to imitate _____.

SP17 James 4:7-10 "Therefore, **submit** to God. **Resist** the devil and he will flee from me. **Draw near** to God, and He will draw near to you. **Cleanse** your hands, you sinners; and **purify your hearts**, you double-minded. **Lament and mourn and weep**! Let your laughter be turned to mourning and your joy to gloom. **Humble yourselves** in the sight of the Lord, and He will lift you up."

5-3) God's Word requires that I submit to HIM.

5-4) Submission with a contentious Spirit is NOT true Biblical submission.

SP18 Ephesians 5:21-32 The marriage relationship is to reflect the relationship between Jesus Christ and the church. It should include: submission, service, and laying down MY life for my spouse.

5-5) My marriage is a covenant (not a contract) before the Lord, (not a court) to a lifetime of companionship and mutual help.

5-6) My love for my spouse is not to be based on my emotions/feelings, circumstances, or my spouse's responses.

Submissiveness is shown through my denying of self and servanthood.

5-7) Submission is a personal voluntary giving up of myself for another, regardless of how the other person acts

5-8) Submissiveness is shown through my denying of self and servanthood.

HP22 _____ am to live peacefully with _____ men (including my spouse), as much as dependent on _____. Romans 12:18

5-9) What is dependent on me in the marriage relationship?

   a) **Submit to God.** **James 4:7** "Therefore, submit to God. Resist the devil and he will flee from you." NKJV
   b) **Submit to each other. Ephesians 5:21** "Submit to one another in fear of the Lord."

HOW TO have a Godly Marriage:

HP23 My submission must be seen in my conduct.

a) **Wives: Ephesians 5:22** "Wives, submit to your own husbands, as to the Lord." **1 Peter 3:1-6** "Wives, likewise, be submissive to your own husbands, that even if some do not obey the word, they, without a word, may be won by the conduct of their wives, when they observe your chaste conduct accompanied by fear.

b) **Husbands: Ephesians 5:25** "Husbands, love your wives, just as Christ also loved the church and gave Himself for her," **1 Peter 3:7** "Husbands, likewise, dwell with them with understanding, giving honor to the wife, as to the weaker vessel, and as being heirs together of the grace of life, that your prayers may not be hindered."

c) I am show Biblical love and communication - 1 Corinthians 13:4-8 Lesson 4
d) I am to forgive immediately - Matthew 6:15 - Lesson 3
e) I am to go be reconciled – Matthew 5:23 – Lesson 3
f) I am to start restoring the relationship – Romans 12:18 Lesson 3
g) I am to put off anger – Colossians 3:8 - Lesson 2
h) I am to overlook offenses – Proverbs 19:11, Proverbs 17:9
i) My body is not my own – 1 Corinthians 7:1-6

When I do it God's way, it means that I am:

Denying self!!– Luke 9:23-24

AND my part in my marriage will reflect the relationship between

_____

HOPE: 1 Peter 5:10

5-11) WHEN God COMMANDS me to be submissive onto Him and others, **THEN** God has given me the ABILITY to do so _____ of what my spouse does to me and _____ of my feelings.

5-12) WHEN I function the way _____ was created, **THEN** I will experience love, joy, peace, patience, kindness, goodness, _____, _____, and self-control even when I don't feel like being loving to my spouse. Galatians 5:22-25

<u>Notes</u>

Scriptural Memorization

"Your word I have treasured in my heart, That I may not sin against You." Psalm 119:11

"Let the word of Christ richly dwell within you, with all wisdom teaching and admonishing one another with psalms and hymns and spiritual songs, singing with thankfulness in your hearts to God." Colossians 3:16

Scriptural Principles to Memorize:

James 4:7-10   Romans 12:18
Ephesians 5:21

HOW TO Have A Godly Marriage Principles:

Wives: Ephesians 5:22-24, 1 Peter 3:1-6

Husbands: Ephesians 5:25-33, 1 Peter 3:7

Wives and Husbands: Ephesians 5:21, 1 Peter 3:8-12, 1 Corinthians 7:1-6

Also **DO** everything toward your spouse that you have learned in this Bible Study. Put off your anger, forgive quickly, and show love even if you do not feel like it.

Heartwork

1) What is Biblical submission?

2) In what ways have you not submitted to your Heavenly Father?

3) In what ways have you not submitted to your husband/wife? Ephesians 5:21

4) Explain what this means......"the marriage relationship is to reflect the relationship between Jesus Christ and His church".

5) What are wives/husbands instructed to do in the marriage relationship? Wives, write out your instructions. Husbands, write your instructions. Site Scripture. Please do not focus on your spouse's part, you are to focus on yours alone.

6) What are some of the ways in which you demonstrate that you are filled with the Holy Spirit (under the control of the Holy Spirit). HINT: Ephesians 5:19,20, 21,22 and 25.

7) Write out what is dependent on you in your marriage that we have learned so far in this class.

8) How can you make your marriage/relationship better?

9) How can you instruct "younger women/men" on marriage?

In-Class Notes
Lesson 6: How Do I Have Peaceful Relationships With My Children?

The Purpose: this lesson takes a different look at our roles as parents. We learn about our "gifts" and what we are to do with these gifts. This class is for parents of young children as well as parents of adult children.

Psalm 127:3-4	Psalm 24:1
Proverbs 22:6	Isaiah 55:11
Ephesians 5:20	Deuteronomy 6:6-7
Matthew 28:18-20	James 5:16
John 13:1-17	Acts 2:1-47
Ephesians 6:1-4	

SP – Scriptural Principle   HP – HOW TO Principle

SP19 Psalm 127:3 (NLT) "Children are a gift from the Lord; they are a reward from Him."

SP20 Psalm 24:1 "The earth is the Lord's, and all its fullness, the world and those who dwell therein."

6-1) Who and what I think of my children affects HOW I respond to my children because my view of self affects how I approach all relationships and problems in life.

SP21 Proverbs 22:6 "Train up a child in the way he should go, And when he is old he will not depart from it." We should "train them in the way they should go" because they are arrows and will not stay in the quiver. Psalm 127:4

SP22 Ephesians 6:4b (NLT) "...bring them up with the discipline and instruction that comes from the Lord."

6-2) What does God want us to do with these gifts?

_____

6-3) My purpose and responsibility of parenting is to be a faithful steward of teaching my arrows God's Word.

SP23 Ephesians 6:4 I am NOT to provoke my gifts. I provoke them when I **do not:** deny self, carry my cross daily, follow Jesus, put off lashing out in anger, put of unforgiveness, and show Biblical love (see Lesson 4).

<u>HOW TO Have Peaceful Relationships With My Children</u>

Our commitment to our children is to be:

HP24 Godly Examples - Duet.4:9, 6:8-9, Matthew 18:5-7, 1 Corinthians 4:14-16
HP25 Godly Servants - 1 Corinthians 13:4-8a, 2 Corinthians 12:14, Philippians 2:3-4
HP26 Godly Disciples - Proverbs 15:10, 2 Timothy 2:24-26

6-4) My discipleship to God's children should be with the focus to submit to God's Word **in my own life**. I need to be a good example, so they submit to God's Word, not mine, when then leave my home.

6-5) You may have a tense relationship when your older children leave your home or are still living with you because you may not have trained them and instructed them **by** your Godly example, your Godly servanthood, or your Godly Discipleship. When you are not a Godly example, servant, or disciple, you can provoke your children to anger. That anger may be taken out on you because you failed to deny self, put off your anger, forgive quickly, and showed love regardless of how you feel while your children were in your care (lived with you).

HOW TO reconcile with older children:

HP27 Change the way you think about your relationship with your children. If your children are believers, they are your brother and/or sisters in Christ. If they are non-believers, you are commanded to "love your enemies" by **DOING** all you have learned toward them. You may not be the one God uses to bring your children to Him. You had your chance while they were in your care.

HP28 If there is tension:
    A. Self-examine – Matthew 7:1-5
    B. Confess to God – Proverbs 28:13
    C. **DO** Mark 11:25 & Matthew 5:23-24
    D. Start acting lovingly, 1 Corinthians 13:4-8
        1. Get to know them
        2. Do for them
        3. Stop being judgmental
        4. **Do not** give counsel unless they ask (they
        will only receive this as you being contentious).

HOPE: Joel 2:25 God can restore broken relationships, if that is His will.

6-6) WHEN God commands me NOT to provoke His children, **THEN** God has given _____ the ability to do so.

6-7) WHEN I function the way I was created, **THEN** I will have love, joy, peace, patience, kindness, _____,

_____, _____,

and _____. Galatians 5:22-25

<u>Notes</u>

Scriptural Memorization

"Your word I have treasured in my heart, That I may not sin against You." Psalm 119:11

"Let the word of Christ richly dwell within you, with all wisdom teaching and admonishing one another with psalms and hymns and spiritual songs, singing with thankfulness in your hearts to God." Colossians 3:16

Scriptural Principles to Memorize:

Psalm 127:3   Psalm 24:1
Proverbs 22:6

HOW TO Have Peaceful Relations with Children Principles:

Ephesians 6:4   1 Corinthians 13:4-8
Proverbs 15:10

Heartwork

1) Has your view of parenting changed after gaining more Biblical understanding? Explain

2) What is your purpose and responsibility as a person gifted with children?

3) In what three ways are we to train our children? We are to be:

4) Do you have peacefully relationships with all your children?

5) List the children you do not have a peaceful relationship with?

6) Have you done all that is "dependent on you" in this relationship? Explain. Be specific. Think about all we have learned: anger, forgiveness, reconciliation, showing biblical love and communicating biblically, being a Godly: example, servant, and disciple.

7) What verse(s) can you use to renew your mind to help you reconcile this relationship?

8) Write out a plan to help you overcome, deal with, and endure this broken relationship. Use a My Victory Plan sheet

9) Write out Joel 2:25 and explain what that means. Do you believe that?

In-Class Notes
Lesson 7: How Can I Put On Biblical Boundaries?

The Purpose: to understand that when we are completely obedient to some of His instructions, the boundaries are set.

Proverbs 4:23	1 Thessalonians 5:19
Matthew 10:34-38	Romans 3:23
2 John 1:10-11	Proverbs 4:14-15, 14:7
Proverbs 22:24-25	Galatians 4:16
Isaiah 41:20	Proverbs 4:1-2, 4-5
Mark 7:15	Proverbs 22:10
Ephesians 4:15	Matthew 5:37
Proverbs 19:11	Proverbs 10:19
2 Timothy 3:1-5	James 4:17
Matthew 11:28-30	2 Corinthians 6:14-16
Hebrews 12:11-13	Deuteronomy 13:1-11

SP – Scriptural Principle   HP – HOW TO Principle

SP28 Proverbs 4:23(NIV) "Above all else, guard your heart, for everything you do flows from it."
1 Thessalonians 5:19(AMP) "Do not quench [subdue, or be unresponsive to the working and guidance of] the [Holy] Spirit."

9-1) Biblical Boundaries are to help us "guard our hearts" and "not quench the Spirit" so that we stay functioning in HIS Spirit. This is how we spread the Gospel. Biblical Boundaries are not to be used as a form of punishment.

SP29 Matthew 10:34-38 Jesus did not come to bring peace. He came to bring a sword which will cause division.

9-2) Jesus's coming, in and of itself, brought division.
- ➢ Division brings conflict between:
- ➢ Good & Evil
- ➢ Light & Darkness
- ➢ Children of God & Children of the Devil
- ➢ Righteousness & Lawlessness
- ➢ Flesh & Spirit

9-3) God, through His Word has given us knowledge and Spiritual discernment on what a fool is and what we are to do with a repeated fools in our lives.
- ➢ Hates knowledge (Proverbs 1:22)
- ➢ Takes no pleasure in understanding (Proverbs 18:2)
- ➢ Enjoys wicked schemes (Proverbs 10:23)
- ➢ Speaks perversity (Proverbs 19:1)
- ➢ Is quick tempered (Proverbs 12:16)
- ➢ Gets self into trouble with proud speech (Proverbs 14:3)
- ➢ Mocks sin (Proverbs 14:9)
- ➢ Is deceitful (Proverbs 14:8)
- ➢ Despises his mother (Proverbs 15:20)
- ➢ Foolish man commits sexual immorality (Proverbs 6:32, 7:7-12)

➢ Foolish woman tears down her own house (Proverbs14:1)

SP30 Romans 3:23 I will still continue to stumble and fall.

9-4) I am MY own stumbling block. 2 John 1:10-11

9-5) Why do I stumble? Proverbs 4:14-15, Proverbs 14:7, Proverbs 22:24-25

9-6) I am commanded to guard my heart. Proverbs 4:23

9-7) I am commanded NOT to quench the Spirit. 1 Thessalonians 5:19

9-8) When I do not do these things, I am causing myself to stumble
.

<u>HOW TO Put On Biblical Boundaries</u> - to keep ME functioning in the Spirit. Biblical Boundaries are NOT to punish others.
HP36 2 Timothy 3:1-5 TURN FROM SELF by denying self (Luke 9:23-24)
HP37 Ephesians 4:15 "Speak truth in love"
HP38 Matthew 5:37 "Let your Yes be Yes and your No be No"
H39 Proverbs 19:11 "Overlook offenses"
HP40 Proverbs 10:19 "Restrain your words"
HP41 2 Timothy 2:23 "Avoid foolish arguments"

MAYBE try:
HP42 Matthew 18**:15**, Galatians 6:1 Restoring another believer IF you have put off your anger, have forgiven, and can communicate with Biblical love.

IF YOU CONTINUE TO STUMBLE:
HP43 2 Timothy 3:1-5 "Turn from such people"   , Proverbs 22:10 "Cast out the scoffer, and contention will leave; Yes, strife and reproach will cease."

Proverbs 4:14-15 "Do not enter the path of the wicked, And do not walk in the way of evil. Avoid it, do not travel on it; Turn away from it and pass on."

9-9) God has established boundaries from the very beginning. It is okay and expected by God that you "guard your heart" and "do not quench" His Spirit that is in you. That may mean turning from such people. It doesn't mean forever. When you have done your part and done all the Lord has commanded, you are right with God. While being "turned away" from "such people", you are still required to apply all that you have learned.

> ➢ Genesis 2:16-17
> ➢ Exodus 20:1-17
> ➢ Deuteronomy 13, 14:1-2

HOPE: Romans 8:28-29

9-10) WHEN God commands me to "turn from such people", **THEN** God has given me the ability to do so. I can "turn away/cast out" people in my life, in peace, if I have done what is dependent on me.

9-11) WHEN I function the way I was created, in love, **THEN** I will have love, joy, _____, patience, goodness, _____, _____, faithfulness, and _____ even when I have to do the hard command of "turning away/casting out" those in my life whom I cannot function in the Spirit with.

<u>Notes</u>

<u>Scriptural Memorization</u>

Psalm 119:11   **Colossians 3:16**

Scriptural Memorization is the Christian's tool in having victory over the temptation to sin. When you have His Word implanted in your heart, He will bring them into your remembrance when you are in trials. When you memorize His Word you are well equipped to have VICTORY in your life. These are great to memorize.

Scriptural Principles to Memorize:
> Proverbs 4:23   1 Thessalonians 5:19
> Romans 3:23

HOW TO Put On Biblical Boundaries Principles:
> Pick some from HP36 – HP43

Heartwork

1) Why does God command that we "guard our hearts" in Proverbs 4:23 and not to "quench the Spirit" in 1 Thessalonians 5:19?

2) How have you been your own stumbling block in regards to your interpersonal relationships? How?

3) What is your plan to live peacefully with all men?

4) Are boundaries okay? Is it okay to "turn from such people"? Why?

5) Does God say to turn from such people forever? When do you know when it is time to start restoring this relationship once you have cast others out?

6) Fill out a My Victory Plan and do it.

In-Class Notes
Lesson 8: How Do I Put Off My Fear, Worry, and Anxiousness?

The Purpose: this lesson teaches us where our fear, worry, anxiousness, and stress arise from. This class will show you how to overcome fear, worry, anxiousness, and stress in the only real way.

Colossians 3:2	Philippians 4:6-9
2 Corinthians 10:5-6	Ephesians 4:27
Matthew 5:28	John 3:15
Matthew 6:33-34	1 John 4:18
I John 4:17-18	2 Timothy 1:7
John 1:9	James 5:16
I Corinthians 10:13	

SP – Scriptural Principle   HP – HOW TO Principle

SP24 Colossians 3:2, Philippians 4:6-9, 2Corinthians 10:5-6
The Bible admonishes (to urge to a duty; remind) me correct my thought life.

7-1) It is an important part of my Christian walk that I eliminate sinful thought patterns, especially the ones which the world has deemed normal; fear, worry, anxiousness, stress, and sometimes depression.

7-2) When do I have feelings of fear or worry?

7-3) Fear and worry are typically centered on some perceived unpleasant experience that may happen in the future. They could arise because of what I have experienced in the past.

SP25 Ephesians 4:27 "…and do not give the devil a foothold."

7-4) A foothold can be described as an intruder that has one foot in your front door while you are attempting to push the door shut and lock it so he cannot enter. If the Devil has a foothold in your life, it is quite easy to overcome it when functioning in His Spirit and slam the door. If the Devil is allowed to push open the door and come into your home, he now has a stronghold.

7-5) If I have a stronghold of an incorrect way of thinking that has molded itself into my way of thinking; it has the capability to affect my feelings, how I respond to various situations in life, and they can play a large role in my spiritual freedom. I am giving the Devil more opportunities to tempt me to sin. He has another foothold (opportunity, a place) in my life.

7-6) When _____ let fear and worry overcome me; I am really showing that I do not love God.

- I am showing that _____ want to control my life.
- I am showing that _____ do not trust Him.

7-7) _____ was **NOT** created to function in control of others, circumstances, or situations. That is _____ job.

HOW TO overcome fear, worry, stress, anxiousness:

HP29 2 Corinthians 10:3-6

HP30 Matthew 6:33-34

HP31 Philippians 4:6-9 Overcoming ALL my battles, especially with fear, worry, and anxiousness are not just in prayer but also a matter of **practicing and controlling** my thought life.

7-8) Showing love MEANS letting God be who HE is (in control of everything) and following all His commands for my life.

HOPE: Isaiah 55:8-9

7-9) WHEN God commands _____ NOT to fear, worry, or be anxious **THEN** God has given _____ the ability to do so!

7-10) WHEN I function the way I was created, **THEN** I will experience love, joy, peace, patience, _____,

_____, _____,

_____, and _____ in

my life. Galatians 5:22-25

Notes

Scriptural Memorization

"Your word I have treasured in my heart, That I may not sin against You." Psalm 119:11

"Let the word of Christ richly dwell within you, with all wisdom teaching and admonishing one another with psalms and hymns and spiritual songs, singing with thankfulness in your hearts to God." Colossians 3:16

Scriptural Principals to Memorize:

Colossians 3:2   2 Timothy 1:7

HOW TO Put Off Fear, Worry, Anxiousness Principles:

2 Corinthians 10:3-6 (How do you do this? By doing Philippians 4:6-9 and Mathew 6:33-34)

Philippians 4:6-9

Matthew 6:33-34

<u>Heartwork</u>

1) Explain what 1 John 4:18 means?

2) What is a stronghold and a foothold?

3) Do you have a stronghold?

4) Are you giving the Devil a foothold in your life?

5) How can you link a "preoccupation with self" with fear, worry, stress, and depression?

6) Write out Matthew 6:26-34. What does this mean? And how does this bring you comfort?

7) How will you overcome feelings of fear, worry, and stress?

Site scripture-try and find more in the Bible other than Phil 4:6-8

8) Develop a plan to overcome your fear or worry by doing a My Victory Plan Over Sin, Death, and the Devil. Instructions found on page 125.

In-Class Notes
Lesson 9: How Do I Put Off Debilitating Grief and Depression?

The Purpose: this lesson will show that no one is immune from the feelings of grief and depression. While in grief and depression, God still requires us to act Biblically in our thoughts, words, and actions. We will learn how to do that.

Matthew 27:1-5	Psalm 38
Jonah 4:1-11	1 Kings 19:4
James 5:17	Romans 12:1
Psalm 139:1-14	Ecclesiastes 7:2-4
Ecclesiastes3:1-8	Genesis 4:1-8
Ephesians 5:15-16	Luke 16:10
2Corinthians1:3-5	1 Kings 17:1-7
Colossians 3:23-24	

SP-Scriptural Principle   HP-HOW TO Principle

8-1) _____ am not completely immune from feelings of depression.

8-2) Some well know people from the Bible experienced feelings of depression:

- Judas - Matthew 27:1-5
- David - Psalm 38
- Jonah - Jonah 4:1-11
- Peter - Matthew 26:69-75
- Elijah - 1 Kings 19:4
- Disciples -

8-3) Feelings of depression can have three triggers: circumstantial, behavioral, and physiological.

SP26 Psalm 38:3-7 My emotions and physical symptoms of depression are not identified as sin in the Bible. But, during grief and depression, my responses to situations and relationships may be identified as sin, depending, again, on whether the focus of my heart is on pleasing self or on pleasing God.

8-4) _____ still responsible to respond Biblically (in His Spirit) in any difficulty regardless of my feelings, even if those are feelings of grief and/or depression.

SP27 1 Corinthians 10:13 God is sovereign and will never allow a circumstance or problem to come into _____ life that would make it impossible for _____ to be obedient to His Word.

8-5) Mourning can turn into feelings of depression when I AM not fulfilling my responsibilities and when I am looking more inward (preoccupation of self) than on God.

8-6) _____ need to be obedient oriented, not feeling oriented. A depressed person allows feelings to lead his/her life. The problem is not a lack of understanding or capability. The issue is the willingness to do God's will and faithfulness in doing it.

HOW TO overcome debilitating grief and depression:

HP32 Genesis 4:7 "If you do well, will you not be accepted? And if you do not do well, sin lies at the door. And its desire *is* for you, but you should rule over it." When you do not do your responsibilities and do them well, you are giving the Devil a foothold.

HP33 Romans 6:11-13, 19; 1 Timothy 4:7-11 "Put off" disobedience to God's Word and "Put On" living a disciplined, faithfully obedient life out of a commitment to please God instead of yourself. (2 Corinthians 5:14-15, Galatians 5:16-17)

HP34 Ephesians 5:15-17, James 4:17 "Establish a biblical schedule for fulfilling your God-given responsibilities and keep the schedule regardless of any feelings of depression you may experience. " Biblical Counseling Foundation. **It is essential that you fill out a My Victory Plan and do it daily.**

HP35 Matthew 5:16, 1 Corinthians 10:31, Colossians 3:17, 23-24 Do all your responsibilities and tasks heartily as to the Lord and for His glory.

HP40 1 John 1:9 If you sin, confess this to the Lord.

HOPE: Romans 15:13

8-7) WHEN God COMMANDS that I be obedient oriented and not feelings oriented, **THEN** _____ has given me the ability to do so regardless of my feelings of grief and depression.

8-8) WHEN _____ function the way I was created, in _____, **THEN** I will have love, joy, peace,

_____,

_____,

_____,

_____,

_____,

_____. Galatians 5:22-25

Notes

Scriptural Memorization

Psalm 119:11   Colossians 3:16

Scriptural Memorization is the Christian's tool in having victory over the temptation to sin. When you have His Word implanted in your heart, He will bring them into your remembrance when you are in trials. When you memorize His Word you are well equipped to have VICTORY in your life. These are great verse to memorize.

Scriptural Principles to Memorize:

Ecclesiastes 7:2-4   Ecclesiastes 3:1-8

HOW TO Put Off Grief and Depression Principles:

Genesis 4:7

Pick one How To Principle HP36 – HP40
(page 83 & 84)

Heartwork

1) What issues in my life cause me to grieve? Is mourning and grieving okay? If so, why? Ecclesiastes 3:1-8

2) How can Ecclesiastes 3:1-8 give you some hope for your grief?

3) Have you been depressed? Explain.

4) What are you responsible for during your feelings of depression?

5) How can you still "do well" during your feelings of depression.

6) Fill out a My Victory Plan and Do it.

7) Additional study. Research King David's fall www.gotquestions.org/David-and-Bathsheba.html , or http://www.case-studies.com/david1 or Elijah www.nuggetsoftruth.com/dealing_with_depression.htm

In-Class Notes
Lesson 10: How Do I Put Off Life Dominating Sins?

The Purpose: in this lesson we explore what life dominating sins really are.

Romans 7:24-25	Ephesians 5:15-18
1 Corinthians 6:9-10	Galatians 5:19-20
John 3:4, 3:8-10	Romans 6:16-18
Psalm 66:18	Proverbs 15:29
Isaiah 59:1-2	1 Peter 3:12
Psalm 32:3-5	Psalm 51:8-12
2 Corinthians 11:14-15	
Matthew 12:26-29	Romans 8:35-39
John 5:19b	Exodus 20:4-6

SP – Scriptural Principle   HP – HOW TO Principle

10-1) We have heard that the philosophy of this world often teaches that undesirable behavior (what the Bible names as sin) is caused by a "disease" or a "predisposition" which we learn to "cope" with.

10-2) When people say they are genetically predisposed to drunkenness or addictions or sexually immorality of any kind, what they are saying is that God gave them a gene that makes it so and since God made us with a gene to be a drunkard, or have additions, or any sexual immoralities, it is embedded in our DNA and we have no choice but to be that way.

10-3) Does God create us to live a life of sin? Ask yourself these questions

- Does God favor one man over the other? God does not give one person the ability to be obedient and make another with the inability to be obedient. Romans 2:11, Col. 3:25, James 2:1, 1 Peter 1:17.
- Does god require/command the impossible? No. John 4:7-16, Ephesians 2:4-8, 1 Corinthians 10:13
- Is God always just? Yes, the justice is always the same. Duet. 32:4, 2 Chron. 19:7, 2 Thess. 1:6, Romans 9:14, Acts 1:34-35
- Sin results from what? You choosing to give into the temptation. Galatians 6:7-8, James 1:14-15, Romans 6:16-18, Romans 8:5-13
- Who is man predestined to seek? Acts 17:26-27, Romans 1:18-21, 24-27, 28, 32

SP31 Ephesians 5:18 When I am willingly or unknowingly under the control of any power other than God's Holy Spirit _____ am in bondage to sin.

SP32 1 John 3:9-10 Life-dominating sin is not the severity or nature of the sin but rather the repeated practice of any sin.

10-4) "Life Dominating Sin Characteristics (fill in with "I").

- _____ practice this sin even though _____ have repeatedly tried to stop.
- _____ practice this sin and blame others or circumstances for _____ failure to stop.
- _____ deny that what _____ am doing is sin.
- _____ convince myself that I am not enslaved to this sin and can stop at any time even though I continue to sin.
- _____ convince myself that sin has no power over me since _____ do not commit this sin as much as _____ once did.
- _____ seek to hide my sin.
- _____ revile or slander the very people who are seeking to restore me to the Lord.
- _____ continue in this sin although _____ know that it is not edifying to do so.
- _____ still continue in this sin although _____ know that it obscures the testimony of Jesus in my life and is a stumbling block to others.
- _____ continue in this sin despite the knowledge that God's Word tells me to stop sinning and that God's provision are sufficient to release me from this bondage.
- _____ repeatedly commit this sin while knowing that it does not please the Lord nor bring glory to God.
- _____ continue in this sin even though _____ realize that your deeds (TWA) do not conform to the character of Christ." (taken from the Biblical Counseling Foundation)

10-5) What are your life-dominating sins?

10-6) "Some results of remaining enslaved by MY sin:

- God does not assure _____ that He will hear or answer _____ prayers. (Psalm 66:18)
- _____ will bear spiritual as well as physical consequences. (Psalm 32:3-5, 38:1-10)
- _____ will lose the joy of _____ salvation, _____ relationship with the Lord. (1 John 1:4)
- _____ will become more miserable, life will become more difficult since _____ am giving Satan an advantage in your life 2 Corinthians 2:10-11
- _____ place myself under the corrective discipline of the Lord and the sternness of the discipline to restore me to the Lord and others will increase. (Hebrews 12:5-11)
- _____, through my own deeds, will hinder all true fellowship with those in the body of Christ. (1 Corinthians 5:9-11)
- _____ remain in spiritual delusion because _____ am merely a hearer of the Word and not a doer, (James 1:22-24) and _____ cannot discern clearly between good and evil. (Hebrews 5:14)" Taken from the Biblical Counseling Foundation

10-7) Can we lose salvation? Bible never says we can lose salvation. It says we can lose the "joy of our salvation." Psalm 51:1-12 Instead, Philippians 2:12-13 says to

_____.

SP33 2 Corinthians 5:17 A Christian is a new creation. "Therefore, if anyone is in Christ, he is a new creation; the old has gone, the new has come!" A Christian is not simply an "improved/changed" version of a person; a Christian is an entirely new creature. He is "in Christ."

For a Christian to lose salvation, the new creation would have to be destroyed.

SP34 1 Peter 1:18-19 A Christian is redeemed. "For you know that it was not with perishable things such as silver or gold that you were redeemed from the empty way of life handed down to you from your forefathers, but with the precious blood of Christ, a lamb without blemish or defect" The word redeemed refers to a purchase being made, a price being paid. We were purchased at the cost of Christ's death.

For a Christian to lose salvation, God Himself would have to revoke His purchase of the individual for whom He paid with the precious blood of Christ.

SP35 Romans 5:1 A Christian is justified. "Therefore, since we have been justified through faith, we have peace with God through our Lord Jesus Christ" To justify is to declare righteous. All those who receive Jesus as Savior are "declared righteous" by God.

For a Christian to lose salvation, God would have to go back on His Word and "un-declare" what He had previously declared. Those absolved of guilt would have to be tried again and found guilty. God would have to reverse the sentence handed down from the divine bench.

SP36 John 3:16 A Christian is promised eternal life. "For God so loved the world that he gave his one and only Son, that whoever believes in him shall not perish but have eternal life." Eternal life is the promise of spending forever in heaven with God. God promises, "Believe and you will have eternal life."

For a Christian to lose salvation, eternal life would have to be redefined. The Christian is promised to live forever.

SP37 Ephesians 1:13-14 A Christian is marked by God and sealed by the Spirit. "You also were included in Christ when you heard the message of truth, the gospel of your salvation. When you believed, you were marked in him with a seal, the promised Holy Spirit, who is a deposit guaranteeing our inheritance until the redemption of those who are God's possession—to the praise of his glory." At the moment of faith, the new Christian is marked and sealed with the Spirit, who was promised to act as a deposit to guarantee the heavenly inheritance. The end result is that God's glory is praised.

For a Christian to lose salvation, God would have to erase the mark, withdraw the Spirit, cancel the deposit, break His promise, revoke the guarantee, keep the inheritance, forego the praise, and lessen His glory.

SP38 Romans 8:30 A Christian is guaranteed glorification. "Those he predestined, he also called; those he called, he also justified; those he justified, he also glorified."

For a Christian can lose salvation, then Romans 8:30 is in error, because God could not guarantee glorification for all those whom He predestines, calls, and justifies.

SP39 Romans 11:29 Gifts and the calling to follow Him are irrevocable. "For the gifts and the calling of God are irrevocable." Most, if not all, of what the Bible says happens to us when we receive Christ would be invalidated if salvation could be lost. Salvation is the gift of God, and God's gifts are "irrevocable"

SP40 Titus 1:2 God cannot lie. "…in hope of eternal life which God, who cannot lie, promised before time began," A Christian cannot be un-newly created. The redeemed cannot be unpurchased. Eternal life cannot be temporary. God cannot renege on His Word.

A Christian cannot lose salvation. If sin continues in a believer's life, the question becomes whether he/she was really saved in the first place.

God's Word says:

SP41 Psalm 51:12 "Restore unto me the joy of your salvation."

SP42 Philippians 2:12 "continue to work out your salvation with fear and trembling,"

10-8) "Whenever _____ practice a particular sin, _____ place myself under its control. While enslaved by that sin, _____ cannot legitimately claim to be wholeheartedly following Jesus. If _____ persistently continue to practice this sin and do not take Biblical steps to overcome it, _____ have reason to doubt the genuineness of _____ salvation.

In spite of my own inherent inability to overcome the bondage of a life-dominating sin, God's grace, mercy, and POWER have been provided for me, as a sincere believer in Jesus

Christ, to overcome any sin. Furthermore, as I overcome sin's power by God's enablement, the character of Christ is developed in my life." Biblical Counseling Foundation (based on Romans 6:1-14)

SP43 Ephesians 15-18(AMP) "Therefore see that you walk carefully [living life with honor, purpose, and courage; shunning those who tolerate and enable evil], not as the unwise, but as wise [sensible, intelligent, discerning people], making the very most of your time [on earth, recognizing and taking advantage of each opportunity and using it with wisdom and diligence], because the days are [filled with] evil. Therefore do not be foolish and thoughtless, but understand and firmly grasp what the will of the Lord is. Do not get drunk with wine, for that is wickedness (corruption, stupidity), but be filled with the [Holy] Spirit and constantly guided by Him."

10-9) What is Paul instructing us to do with our lives? Verse 15-16

10-10) How do we do this? Verse 17

10-11) "Most of every opportunity" means that wherever HE places _____, whomever _____ met…. _____ am to spread the Gospel. In Verse 16, you cannot be used to spread the Gospel if you have any life dominating sin (repeated practice of any sin that you have not put a plan in place to overcome Biblically.

HOW TO walk circumspectly and overcome my life dominating sins:

HP44 1 John 1:9 Confess sins to God and repenting (change your behavior). Confession is agreeing with God that you have sinned.

HP45 Ephesians 4:22-24   by filling out a My Victory Plan. You need a plan to help you overcome the temptation to sin. Then you need to **DO** the plan.

HOPE: Isaiah 43:1-2

10-12) WHEN God commands me to put off any sin, including a life dominating sin, **THEN** HE has given me the ability to do so!!

9-13) WHEN I function the way I was created, in LOVE, **THEN** I will experience _____, _____,

_____, _____, _____,

_____, _____,

_____, and

_____ (Galatians 5:22) in my life and I will be completely empowered by the Holy Spirit to overcome any temptation to sin!

<u>Notes</u>

Scriptural Memorization

Psalm 119:11   **Colossians 3:16**

Scriptural Memorization is the Christian's tool in having victory over the temptation to sin. When you have His Word implanted in your heart, He will bring them into your remembrance when you are in trials. When you memorize His Word you are well equipped to have VICTORY in your life. These are great to memorize.

Scriptural Principals to Memorize:

Romans 7:24-25   Ephesians 5:15-18

1 John 3:9-10   2 Corinthians 5:17

HOW TO Put Off My Life Dominating Sins Principles:

1 John 1:9   Ephesians 4:22-24

Heartwork

1) What is a life-dominating sin? Use Scripture and then in your own words

2) What does "do not be drunk with wine" mean?

3) How and when are you drunk with wine?

4) What was one of Jesus' purposes for coming to earth? 1 John 3:8

5) How did Jesus take away Satan's power of death? Hebrews 2:14-15

6) What is the full armor of God? List the six pieces of armor we are to put on and describe each. Ephesians 6:14-17

In-Class Notes
Lesson 11: Am I Really An Overcomer?

The Purpose: this lesson you will learn why you, Christian, can function in the "new creation" and why you are already VICTORIOUS over sin, death and the Devil!

Romans 7:24-25	Isaiah 45:2
Colossians 2:6-7	2 Timothy 3:16-17
Colossians 1:9-10	Matthew 7:1-5
Romans 6:11-14	Ephesians 4:22-24
1 John 5:4-5	Matthew 28:19-20
1 Corinthians 11:28	

SP – Scriptural Principle   HP – HOW TO Principle

11-1) After you receive salvation by God's grace through our Lord Jesus Christ, your GROWTH and FITNESS to help others biblically will be in proportion to your faithfulness in biblically examining yourself and applying God's Truths to your life." Biblical Counseling Foundation

SP44 Acts 4:12 "Nor is there salvation in any other, for there is no other name under heaven given among men by which we must be saved."

Because of His death and resurrection:

The Lord Jesus Christ is victorious over SIN!

SP45 Romans 6:10 "For the death that He died, He died to sin once for all; but the life that He lives, He lives to God."

Because of His death and resurrection:

The Lord Jesus Christ is victorious over DEATH!

SP46 Romans 6:9 "Knowing that Christ, having been raised from the dead, dies no more. Death no longer has dominion over Him.

Because of His death and resurrection:

The Lord Jesus Christ is victorious over the DEVIL!

SP47 Hebrews 2:14 "Inasmuch then as the children have partaken of flesh and blood, He Himself likewise shared in the same, that through death He might destroy him who had the power of death, that is, the devil!"

11-2) Since we know that once we are born again, His Spirit is in us and since Jesus is already victorious over SIN, DEATH, AND THE DEVIL, who can also be victorious over SIN, DEATH, AND THE DEVIL too?

_____!!!!!!

BUT...I have to choose righteousness. I have to choose to function in His Spirit rather than in my flesh. That is the only place where the battle of the flesh vs. Spirit is won.

11-3) In order to function in the "new creation", I need to:

- Establish a Biblical pattern of life
- Prepare myself to help others

11-4) Three resources given to me from God at Salvation:

- **The Bible** - I can understand it.
- **The Holy Spirit** – empowers me to overcome.
- **Prayer** – provides communication with God.

SP48 1 Corinthians 11:28 A commitment to please God begins when I self-exam.

HOW TO function in the "new creation" Ultimate How Principle:

HP6 Ephesians 4:22-24 was introduced in Lesson 2 (Book 2). It is the only method needed to overcome, deal with, and/or endure all problems in your life.

"that you put off, concerning your former conduct, the old man which grows corrupt according to the deceitful lusts".
Ephesians 4:22

In order to know what "old man" behaviors to put off", you need to self-exam your thoughts, words, and actions according to God's standards.

"and be renewed in the spirit of your mind, "
Ephesians 4:23

11-5) I renew my mind by:

- **listening to the Word** being preached or a teaching from God's Word. (Romans 10:17)
- **having daily readings** in the Word. (1 Timothy 4:13)
- **investigating the Word** and learning scripturally based principles of living. (2 Timothy 2:15)

- **reviewing memory verse** cards throughout the day. (Psalm 119:11)
- **thinking of the personal application** of God's promise and commands to you. (Joshua 1:8, Psalm 1:2)
- **implementing your plans** in all areas of your life. (James 1:22)

AND THAT:

"…...you put on the new man which was created according to God, in true righteousness and holiness."

You need to make the conscious effort to "put off" your "old man" habits and instead "put on" the "new creation" habits.

By doing the above, I provide opportunities for the Word of Christ to dwell in me and to create "new creation" living. New creation living means to be walking in His Spirit. We are walking in His Spirit by DOING what God commands.

SP49 2 Corinthians 5:17- 21 "Therefore, if anyone is in Christ, the new creation has come: The old has gone, the new is here! All this is from God, who reconciled us to himself through Christ and gave us the ministry of reconciliation: that God was reconciling the world to himself in Christ, not counting people's sins against them. And he has committed to us the message of reconciliation. We are therefore Christ's ambassadors, as though God were making his appeal through us. We implore you on Christ's behalf: Be reconciled to God. God made him who had no sin to be sin for us, so that in him we might become the righteousness of God."

HOPE: 2 Corinthians 4:17-18

11-6) WHEN God commands me to repent (change-from reacting in the old man to responding in the new creation), **THEN** HE has given me the ability to do so! But it is only by the power of the Holy Spirit. I have that power only by being obedient to His Word.

11-7) WHEN I function the way I was created, **THEN** I will have _____, _____, _____, _____,

_____, _____,

_____, _____, and

_____ spilling out of me when shaken. It is then and only then that I will experience the "abundant life" God promises me!

I am an overcomer,

"Who is the one who is victorious and overcomes the world?" 1 John 5:5

It is the one who believes and recognizes the fact that Jesus is the Son of God." 1 John 5:5

I just need to act like it!

For the [true] love of God is this: that we habitually keep His commandments and remain focused on His precepts. And His commandments and His precepts are not difficult [to obey]. For everyone born of God is victorious and overcomes the world; and this is the victory that has conquered and overcome the world—our [continuing, persistent] faith [in Jesus the Son of God'. 1 John 5:3-4

<u>Notes</u>

<u>Scriptural Memorization</u>

Psalm 119:11   Colossians 3:16

Scriptural Memorization is the Christian's tool in having victory over the temptation to sin. When you have His Word implanted in your heart, He will bring them into your remembrance when you are in trials. When you memorize His Word you are well equipped to have VICTORY in your life. These are essential verses to memorize.

<u>Scriptural Principles to Memorize:</u>

2 Timothy 3:16-17   Matthew 7:1-5

<u>HOW TO Be An Overcomer Principles:</u>

1 Corinthians 11:28   Ephesians 4:22-24

Heartwork

1) Are you an overcomer?

2) Why?

3) What shows that you are?

Review Sheet

Long lasting "new creation" living starts with salvation. This is our goal, to be Christlike.

The Greatest Commandments:

Vertical (God)

Jesus said to him, "'You shall love the Lord your God with all your heart, with all your soul, and with all your mind.'This is the first and great commandment.And the second is like it: 'You shall love your neighbor as yourself.' - Matthew 22:37-39

When there are problems in your horizontal relationships, the real problem is one of obedience in your vertical relationship. Loving the Lord and loving your neighbors are inseparable.

Horizontal (Neighbors)

We fail at loving God and loving

our neighbor because:

"But know this, that in the last days perilous times will come: For men will be lovers of themselves, lovers of money, boasters, proud, blasphemers, disobedient to parents, unthankful, unholy, unloving, unforgiving, slanderers, without self-control, brutal, despisers of good, traitors, headstrong, haughty, lovers of pleasure rather than lovers of God, " 2 Timothy 3:1-4

We are lovers of ourselves.

In order to love God and love our neighbors as ourselves we simply need to reverse our focus from self to others.

The Bible was given to us so that we can be reconciled to God. After the Fall of man in the Garden of Eden, we all became sinners. Accepting Jesus Christ as our Lord and Savior, brought reconciliation between God and ourselves. "Reconciliation involves a change in the relationship between God and man or man and man. It assumes there has been a breakdown in the relationship, but now there has been a change from a state of enmity and fragmentation to one of harmony and fellowship." William J. Woodruff, BibleStudyTools.com. Once that takes place, we are now in the ministry of reconciliation. We do ministry of reconcilation 2 Coritnthains 5:11-21, by going out into the world, preaching the Gospel, making disciples. This can only happen if we "deny self, carry your cross daily, and follow Him."

The Bible is jammed packed with "denying self" verses.

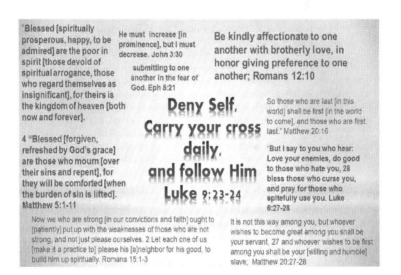

"Blessed [spiritually prosperous, happy, to be admired] are the poor in spirit [those devoid of spiritual arrogance, those who regard themselves as insignificant], for theirs is the kingdom of heaven [both now and forever].

4 "Blessed [forgiven, refreshed by God's grace] are those who mourn [over their sins and repent], for they will be comforted [when the burden of sin is lifted]. Matthew 5:1-11

He must increase [in prominence], but I must decrease. John 3:30

submitting to one another in the fear of God. Eph 5:21

Deny Self.
Carry your cross daily,
and follow Him
Luke 9:23-24

Be kindly affectionate to one another with brotherly love, in honor giving preference to one another; Romans 12:10

So those who are last [in this world] shall be first [in the world to come], and those who are first last." Matthew 20:16

"But I say to you who hear: Love your enemies, do good to those who hate you, 28 bless those who curse you, and pray for those who spitefully use you. Luke 6:27-28

Now we who are strong [in our convictions and faith] ought to [patiently] put up with the weaknesses of those who are not strong, and not just please ourselves. 2 Let each one of us [make it a practice to] please his [a]neighbor for his good, to build him up spiritually. Romans 15:1-3

It is not this way among you, but whoever wishes to become great among you shall be your servant, 27 and whoever wishes to be first among you shall be your [willing and humble] slave; Matthew 20:27-28

How do we deny self, carry our cross daily, and follow Him?

"Put off, concerning your former conduct, the old man which grows corrupt according to the deceitful lusts, and be renewed in the spirit of your mind, and . . . put on the new man which was created according to God, in righteousness and true holiness"
(Ephesians 4:22-24, NKJV).

God has one way to deny self. One method for putting the deeds of the flesh to death. One method for ovrcoming the temption to sin in your life. This is the ulitmate HOW TO live in the new creation verse.

This is what the Flesh vs. Spirit Bible Study has all about.

My Victory Plan

(I did not make up these Victory Plan Sheets. I first learned about them from the Biblical Counseling Foundation Self-Confrontation Manual developed by John C. Broger. I adapted them to fit the needs of those whom I teach.)

On this sheet we will see HOW to work Ephesians 4:22-24. I titled this worksheet My Victory Plan Over Sin, Death, and the Devil because through the death and resurrection of our Lord Jesus Christ, God was victorious over sin, (Romans 6:10), through the death and resurrection of Jesus, God was victorious over death (Romans 6:9), and through the death and resurrection of Jesus, God was victorious over the Devil (Hebrews 2:15).

Since He is living in you, you too can be victorious over sin, death, and the Devil! But we need a plan. God had a plan. I think God had the plan of Jesus dying for our sins before He created the earth. So, if God had a plan, I think a plan is important for us as well. This is our plan in overcoming the temptation to sin in our anger.

You do not need a nicely printed sheet with the title printed across the top for this next part. I would like you to take a sheet of paper, 8 ½ x 11 works well. Place paper on a flat surface and orient it to landscape style. Fold the left side of paper to the edge of the right side. Then fold the folded half to the edge of the right side. Unfold it and you should have a landscape sheet with four columns. Lable the columns.

My Victory Plan Over Sin, Death, and the Devil

Through the death and resurrection of the Lord Jesus Christ, God was victorious over

SIN (Romans 6:10), DEATH (Romans 6:9), and the DEVIL (Hebrews 2:15).

Self-examine 1 Corinthians 11:28, Galatians 6:4	Put off Eph. 4:22	Ephesians 4:22-24 Put on Eph. 4:23-24	MY PLAN Titus 2:11-14
List specific unbiblical T,W,A- not just emotions or attitudes	For each pattern of sin, write one or two verses as a "put off"	List specific biblical verses for each sinful pattern	List SPECIFIC T,W,A that will replace column 1

READ 1 Corinthians 11:28 (AMP), Galatians 6:4 (AMP)

The first column is our self-examination column. This is the first part of verse Ephesians 4:22, this is the put off part. These are the behaviors that do not bring glory to the Lord because these behaviors are flesh; these behaviors are the ones coming from the bottle with the bitter, spoiled unsweetened coffee. In this first column we are going to list our sinful behaviors. These are the PUT OFFs, our "old man" behaviors.

In the summer of 2016, I was teaching this Bible Study in my cousin's Dance Studio. I had to haul everything I needed for the study; monitor, laptop, HDMI cable, extension cords, notebooks, and a few pieces of furniture. We had to drive thirty minutes one way to get to the Dance Studio. This one particular day, after we had set up I went to hook up the laptop to the monitor and I realized I had forgotten to pack the HDMI cable that I needed. I thought, "No problem, I will just call my daughter to bring it to me." She was at home babysitting her little sister. I called. No answer. "No problem." I thought, she is probably in the restroom or something. I called again. No answer. I called again. No answer. "This girl can't even do her job!" As if her job was to be at my beckon call. I called again. No answer. I grunted and thought, "Darn Ava, what is her problem??" "Why doesn't she have her phone with her?" "What is wrong with that girl??" I become short-tempered with my son who was with me. "Let's go!" I said in a high voice. If I had to go myself to get the cable, we needed to leave to get back in time before the study began. In my actions, I gave facial gestures that told everyone I was upset. As I was driving home, I was tempted to speed! Know what I mean? Before I started doing these Victory Plans, those feelings of anger would have surely spilled out onto the other drivers as I drove home in anger and onto my daughter when I got home. I would have walked in anger, said a few choice words, and left even angrier. But I had been working on putting off the "old man" behaviors for a couple of years at this point and by the Spirit I was able to stop from going on the downward spiral of sin and spilling onto others like it has always done. It was hard, I still wanted to be angry and say ugly things to my daughter. I did!

Think about the last time you had an angry outburst. What were your sinful thoughts, words, and actions? Write them down in column one.

See example on next page.

My Victory Plan Over Sin, Death, and the Devil

Through the death and resurrection of the Lord Jesus Christ, God was victorious over

SIN (Romans 6:10), DEATH (Romans 6:9), and the DEVIL (Hebrews 2:15).

Ephesians 4:22-24		
Self-examine 1 Corinthians 11:28, Galatians 6:4	Put off Eph. 4:22	Put on Eph. 4:23-24	MY PLAN Titus 2:11-14

List specific unbiblical
Thoughts, Words, Actions
- not just emotions or
attitudes

-was wondering, "Why
isn't she doing her job"
-I had a crunched up face
- "UGH" after I called
her
- "What is wrong with
that girl,"
- "My day is ruined"
- Slammed things

Be careful not to blameshift in this first column. It does not matter what the circumstance is or who did what to you. You are reacting in your anger because anger is already in your heart. This is an example of blame shifting: "I had sinful thoughts because my daughter didn't answer the phone." I am essentially blaming her. Remember Mark 7:15?

When I was doing my plans on paper, many years ago, it was at this point where my eyes were opened.

- These reactions were the reason I was miserable.
- These reactions were the reason I did not have peaceful relationships with people.
- These reactions were the reason my relationship with God was hindered.
- These reactions were the reason God wasn't using me.

ME! I was the reason for my misery. Do you see that? I always thought circumstance or other people were the reason for my misery, the reason for my sinful reactions. How wrong I was!! This first column is about you looking at your natural man (flesh) in the mirror (James 1:23-25) so that you can do James 1:22! You know how you have sinned because the Holy Spirit leads you to conviction so that repentance can happen. Let the Holy Spirit bring your sins into your memory. Let the Holy Spirit guide you.

READ Psalm 66:18, Isaiah 59:1-2

When you have unconfessed sin and not working on repentance (changing your behavior) in your life, the Lord does not hear you. If He doesn't hear you, the line of communication with God is temporary broken and that is why you can't hear Him and it may feel like He is not answering your prayers.

I encourage you to do this Victory Plan. It may feel uncomfortable, a little odd but it is the only way I found victory. You can do these for ANY problem you have. There are no shortcuts to living in the new creation. Please finish the first column now.

The two middle columns are for the RENEW YOUR MIND part of Ephesians 4:23. This is the part where you research verses that go with the sin you are struggling with. For this lesson we are trying to put off anger.

In Scriptures God gives us what behaviors to put off and which ones to put in their place, the put ons. When we look for those we need to remember that they need to be in the save verse or in the same general vicinity of one other. So this means that for our anger verse, we do not want to find a put off in Ephesians and then a put on in Galatians. Do you know some verses on anger, which have the put off and the put on? I share mine with you, I have two.

READ Colossians 3:8-14

We do not need to use too much brain power to see what the put offs and the put ons are in this verse. What are the put offs and put ons? Do you see them? In verse 8 and 9, we read some put offs; anger, wrath, malice, blasphemy, filthy language, and lying. These are the deeds of the "old man." In verse 10 and 11, God tells us in very general terms what to put on, put on the "new man". This is a very general verse. But God is so good to us, He then tells us HOW TO put on the "new man" in verse 12-14. Put on; tender mercies, kindness, humility, meekness, longsuffering (patience), bearing with one another, forgiving one another, and put on love! Do you see that? So what God is telling you, is that you have gotten use to functioning in the "old man" ways (flesh), and how you get rid of a habit is by replacing it with something else. We are replacing our old man habit with a new habit of functioning in His Spirit!! This is the "doing" part that James 1:22 is talking about in regards to anger. You are to put on the behaviors in Colossians 3:10-14 (put on the new man of tender mercies, kindness, humility, meekness, longsuffering, bearing with one another, and forgive one another) instead of the behaviors in 3:8-9 (put off the old man of anger, wrath, malice, blasphemy, filthy language, do not lie). Do you get it? How wonderful is our Father!

READ James 1:19-20

What are the put offs?? It is an implied put off of "wrath of man (anger)". What are the put ons? Put on "swift to hear, slow to speak, slow to wrath." For me, this verse had me functioning in the "new creation" faster than anything I had tried. In my anger, I never listened to people and I was very quick to speak. I memorized this verse. I had the only tool, Scripture, needed to overcome the temptation to sin. I think of this verse as my SSS verse, Swift, Slow, Slow. Every time feelings of anger would rise up in me, the Lord brought SSS to my mind to make me aware that sinning was right around the corner. That is what Scripture memorization does for you. If you haven't memorized any Scripture, God can't bring them into your memory.

In the second column, you are to write out the put offs in the verses we picked, Colossians 3:8-9 and James 1:20. These are what you are NOT to do the next time you have those feelings of anger. If Gods says, "put off" then we have to recognize them as sins.

In the third column, you are to write out the put ons in the verses we picked, Colossians 3:12-14 and James 1:19 next to the corresponding verses in the second column.

My Victory Plan Over Sin, Death, and the Devil

Through the death and resurrection of the Lord Jesus Christ, God was victorious over

SIN (Romans 6:10), DEATH (Romans 6:9), and the DEVIL (Hebrews 2:15).

Ephesians 4:22-24

Self-examine 1 Corinthians 11:28, Galatians 6:4	Put off Eph. 4:22	Put on Eph. 4:23-24	MY PLAN Titus 2:11-14
List specific unbiblical Thoughts, Words, Actions - not just emotions or attitudes	For each pattern of sin, write one or two verses as a "put off"	List specific verses for each sinful pattern as a "put on"	
-was wondering, "Why isn't she doing her job" -I had a crunched up face	James 1:20 Wrath of man doesn't produce righteousness of God	James 1:19 let every man be swift to hear, slow to speak, slow to wrath	
- "UGH" after I called her - "What is wrong with that girl." - "My day is ruined" - Slammed things	Col. 3:8-9 put off all these: anger, wrath, malice, blasphemy, filthy language out of your mouth, do not lie	Col. 3:12-14 -put on tender mercies, kindness, humility, meekness, longsuffering; bearing with one another, and forgiving one another, put on love	

What are you seeing as you are doing your sheet? I see self. I see Ephesians 4:22-24 come to life. This is application. I see clearly that HIS WORD has my answers to my problem(s). I am seeing that my problem is my problem because I am not denying self. Do you see that?

Did you notice that the Scriptures we picked had nothing to do with making sure the other person followed HIS WORD? These verses didn't say, "make sure so-and-so doesn't sin in their anger." Does it? It doesn't say, "Make sure that the other person puts off malice, flighty language, or they do not blasphemy." Does it? It doesn't. A lot of the times students will bring up, Galatians 6:1.

READ Galatians 6:1 (NLT)

People use this verse as an excuse to point out everyone else's sin. "…you who are spiritual restore such a one in a spirit of gentleness…". Gentleness is part of the fruit of the Spirit. If you are not in His Spirit, you should not be trying to restore someone by pointing out their sin. If you haven't forgiven someone, you should not be trying to restore. If you read the verses before Galatians 6:1, you will notice that Paul talks about walking in His Spirit.

So what do you think the last column is for?

READ Titus 2:11-14

Column 4 is our plan to overcome the temptation to sin in our anger. It is the plan to overcome any sin! The last column is your plan. This is how you are going to have victory!!! But you have to do it!!! Keep doing your plan until the Spirit subconsciously comes out of you. Once you do this sheet a few times, you will have learned to internalize it. You really won't have to do this sheet again and again. It becomes easier. This is HOW TO have victory for sinning in your anger.

The last column is usually the longest and you may need a few sheets of paper for this column. I broke my plan up into sections; thoughts, words, and actions. I have three pictures below; all are the same except the last column.

For my thoughts:

My Victory Plan Over Sin, Death, and the Devil

Through the death and resurrection of the Lord Jesus Christ, God was victorious over

SIN (Romans 6:10), DEATH (Romans 6:9), and the DEVIL (Hebrews 2:15).

Ephesians 4:22-24

Self-examine 1 Corinthians 11:28, Galatians 6:4	Put off Eph. 4:22	Put on Eph. 4:23-24	MY PLAN Titus 2:11-14
List specific unbiblical T,W,A- not just emotions or attitudes	For each pattern of sin, write one or two verses as a "put off"	List specific biblical verses for each sinful pattern	List SPECIFIC T,W,A that will replace column 1
-was wondering, "Why isn't she doing her job" -I had a crunched up face - "UGH" after I called her - "What is wrong with that girl!" - "My day is ruined"	James 1:20 Wrath of man doesn't produce righteousness of God Col. 3:8 put off all these: anger, wrath, malice, blasphemy, filthy language out of your mouth	James 1:19 let every man be swift to hear, slow to speak, slow to wrath Col. 3:12 -put on tender mercies, kindness, humility, meekness, longsuffering; bearing with one another, and forgiving one another	Think Biblically -pray everyday, ask God to help me with my uncaring thoughts, -Confess-if I was unbiblical -memorize James and Colossians.

For my words:

My Victory Plan Over Sin, Death, and the Devil

Through the death and resurrection of the Lord Jesus Christ, God was victorious over SIN (Romans 6:10), DEATH (Romans 6:9), and the DEVIL (Hebrews 2:15).

_____ Ephesians 4:22-24 _____

Self-examine 1 Corinthians 11:28, Galatians 6:4	Put off Eph. 4:22	Put on Eph. 4:23-24	MY PLAN Titus 2:11-14
List specific unbiblical T,W,A- not just emotions or attitudes	For each pattern of sin, write one or two verses as a "put off"	List specific biblical verses for each sinful pattern	List SPECIFIC T,W,A that will replace column 1
-was wondering, "Why isn't she doing her job" -I had a crunched up face - "UGH" after I called her - "What is wrong with that girl." - "My day is ruined"	James 1:20 Wrath of man doesn't produce righteousness of God Col. 3:8 put off all these: anger, wrath, malice, blasphemy, filthy language out of your mouth	James 1:19 let every man be swift to hear, slow to speak, slow to wrath Col. 3:12 -put on tender mercies, kindness, humility, meekness, longsuffering; bearing with one another, and forgiving one another	Speak Biblically LISTEN before I speak, Speak AFTER hearing gathering information, THINK about what comes out of mouth-only to encourage, Speak Truth if necessary

For my actions:

My Victory Plan Over Sin, Death, and the Devil

Through the death and resurrection of the Lord Jesus Christ, God was victorious over SIN (Romans 6:10), DEATH (Romans 6:9), and the DEVIL (Hebrews 2:15).

| | Ephesians 4:22-24 | | |
Self-examine 1 Corinthians 11:28, Galatians 6:4	Put off Eph. 4:22	Put on Eph. 4:23-24	MY PLAN Titus 2:11-14
List specific unbiblical T,W,A- not just emotions or attitudes	For each pattern of sin, write one or two verses as a "put off"	List specific biblical verses for each sinful pattern that will replace column 1	List SPECIFIC T,W,A that will replace column 1
-was wondering, "Why isn't she doing her job" -I had a crunched up face - "UGH" after I called her - "What is wrong with that girl." - "My day is ruined"	James 1:20 Wrath of man doesn't produce righteousness of God Col. 3:8 put off all these: anger, wrath, malice, blasphemy, filthy language out of your mouth	James 1:19 let every man be swift to hear, slow to speak, slow to wrath Col. 3:12 -put on tender mercies, kindness, humility, meekness, longsuffering; bearing with one another, and forgiving one another	<u>ACT Biblically</u> - When I start to feel the strong emotions, I will pull out(walk to) my index card and read. - Breathe, pray - Go to the bathroom

READ Proverbs 21:21 (NIV)

The first time I implemented my plan, I hung it on my refrigerator. I stay home and I am in the kitchen a lot so I hung it there. First part of my plan, I would pray about my temptation to sin, first thing in the morning. I would pray He would help me, pray that I would follow the plan, and pray that HE would open my eyes so that I could view my strong feelings as a red flag. I would also read from my Bible every morning. I wrote James 1:19-20 and Colossians 3:8-12 on index cards and put them around my house. I carried them where ever I went. I practiced saying them. I memorized them. During the day, when those strong angry feelings would rise in me, I would run to my plan and I would READ it. I would read my verses. Am I being a doing? YES. By the time I would finish reading the verses I was calm. His Word stopped the temptation to sin as I was reading the verses. His Word, my only tool, was enough to put the temptation of the flesh to death.

The next time I had angry feelings; I would run to the plan and read it. I would focus on James 1:19 "Swift to hear, Slow to speak, Slow to wrath", and I would do it!!! This step happened several more times, as putting on a new creation habit takes time and practice.

I remember one day in our kitchen, while I was practicing my plan, the Holy Spirit showed up without me having to run to My Victory Plan! One of my kids had spilled something on the floor, a liquid. (I don't even remember what they had spilled). I remember walking over to the area and my three children were standing behind the liquid on the floor, their eyes were big with fear because I always yelled at them when little accidents happened. Well, this time I simply walked up to them, looked at the liquid on the floor then looked up at them and said in a calm voice,

"Okay, someone just needs to clean that up." And I turned around and calmly walked away! I was thinking, "OH MY! I did not just to that??!! How was I able to just walk away and not sin in my anger?" I was in shock that I didn't sin in my anger. It was His Spirit that was able to put my old man deeds of the flesh to death!! In that moment, I choose to function in love, joy, peace, patience, goodness, gentleness, kindness, and self-control BY being obedient to swift to hear, slow to speak, and slow to wrath (James 1:19) and by being obedient to "put on tender mercies, kindness, humility, meekness, longsuffering.." (Colossians 3:12-14). I remember looking back at my kids as I walked away and they still had those big eyes, only this time isn't a look of fear but of shock also. I could see on their faces a look of, "What just happened and what happened to our mother?" Everyone saw the Spirit that day work a miracle!

The next time I had feelings of anger, I wouldn't have to run to my plan. My mind was renewed, changed to respond in the Spirit. I "put on" the "new creation" way to respond to my children instead of reacting in the flesh! His Spirit just spilled out of me SUBCONSCIOUSLY!!! That is freedom!! That is living!!! Before, the flesh just spilled out of me subconsciously (doing it without having to think about it) when I was shaken. I do not want the flesh spilling out of me, I want and commanded by the Lord that His Spirit spill out of me at all times.

Let me just say this here. You may think my problems are no big deal, that your problems at work, with your marriage, with your family are way BIGGER than mine and that your problems are way too big to be dealt with the way I showed you. Let me share with you what use to happen when I reacted in the flesh with this "little" problem of spilled liquid. Let me show you my "old man" and tell me if your "old man" looks similar. In years past, when an incident like this would happen with my children, I would get so mad, I could literally feel my whole body get hot and tense. My eyes would bulge in anger and then my eyes would be squinting as I tried and make my way to the scene of the accident. As I walked to the accident, I would be thinking, "What is wrong with these kids! I have told them what to do a hundred times! I don't need this right now! I don't need this right now!" Then, that anger would spill out onto them. I would yell, belittle them, and I wouldn't stop. I would continue to have anger the whole day. I would be short-tempered with them and my husband and take my anger out on them by the words that I said. It would take me a whole day to calm down over a little bitty accident/incident. I was miserable. Do your problems, no matter how much more bigger they seem than mine, yield the same result? The problems don't matter, the problems aren't the cause of your problem. You are the reason you are miserable because you react in the flesh.

The My Victory Plan Sheets can be used for ANY problem you are facing. The HOW TO principles in this Notebook, if they contain the "put offs" and "put ons", can be used for your 2nd and 3rd column on your Victory Plan. Choose wisely and only about 1 or 2 verses are needed to start functioning in the new creation.

Oh Lord! We are so thankful for Your plans for us. We are thankful for Your instrctions to get us out of any torture we place ouselves in. Help us Lord. Give us the desire to want to truly follow You in all areas of our lives. Direct us to Your Word, not Corrine's or anyone elses, when we practice Your righteousness. Help us experience Your Spirit, Lord. Give us Your wisdom as we start "new creation" functioning. I ask this in Your name, Jesus, Amen.

Made in the USA
Columbia, SC
02 February 2024

31384937R00100